DREAMWORKS
Shark Tale ™
Movie Storybook

SCHOLASTIC

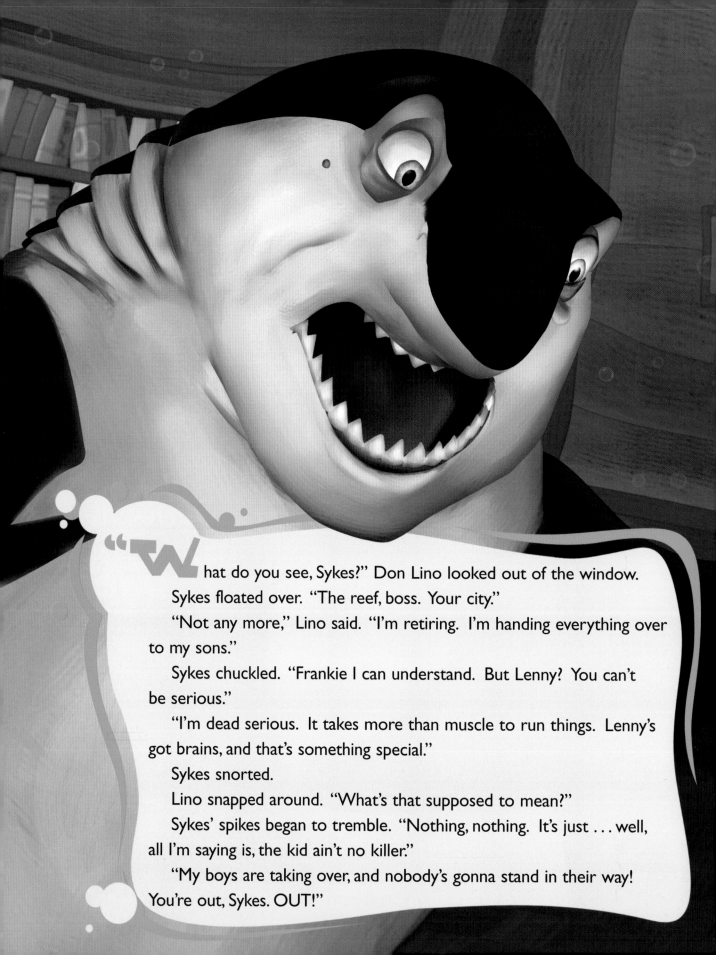

"What do you see, Sykes?" Don Lino looked out of the window.

Sykes floated over. "The reef, boss. Your city."

"Not any more," Lino said. "I'm retiring. I'm handing everything over to my sons."

Sykes chuckled. "Frankie I can understand. But Lenny? You can't be serious."

"I'm dead serious. It takes more than muscle to run things. Lenny's got brains, and that's something special."

Sykes snorted.

Lino snapped around. "What's that supposed to mean?"

Sykes' spikes began to tremble. "Nothing, nothing. It's just . . . well, all I'm saying is, the kid ain't no killer."

"My boys are taking over, and nobody's gonna stand in their way! You're out, Sykes. OUT!"

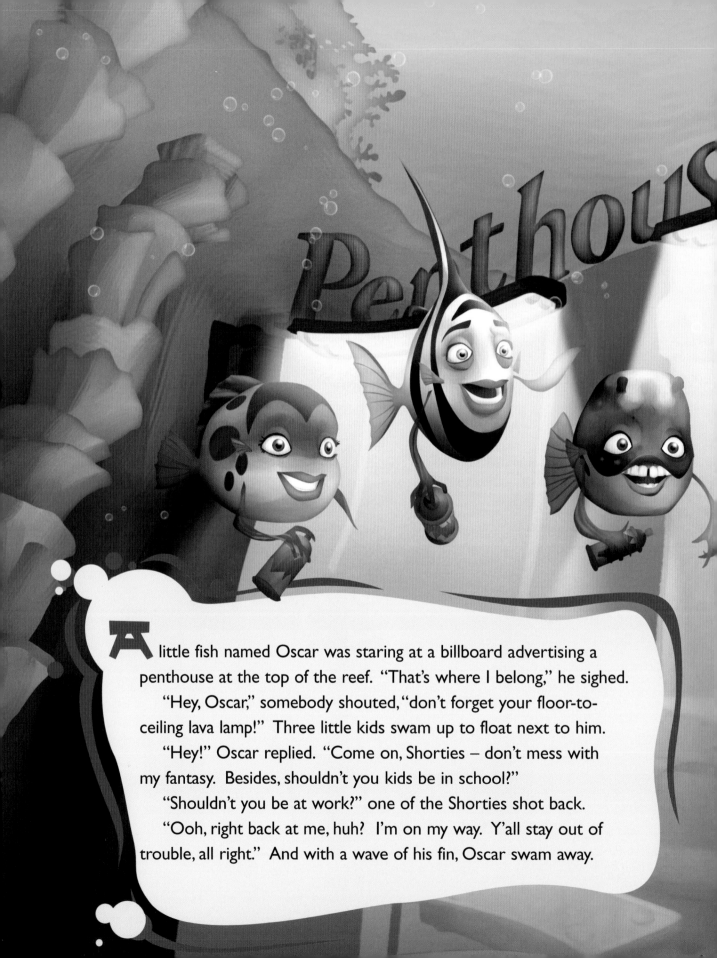

A little fish named Oscar was staring at a billboard advertising a penthouse at the top of the reef. "That's where I belong," he sighed.

"Hey, Oscar," somebody shouted, "don't forget your floor-to-ceiling lava lamp!" Three little kids swam up to float next to him.

"Hey!" Oscar replied. "Come on, Shorties – don't mess with my fantasy. Besides, shouldn't you kids be in school?"

"Shouldn't you be at work?" one of the Shorties shot back.

"Ooh, right back at me, huh? I'm on my way. Y'all stay out of trouble, all right." And with a wave of his fin, Oscar swam away.

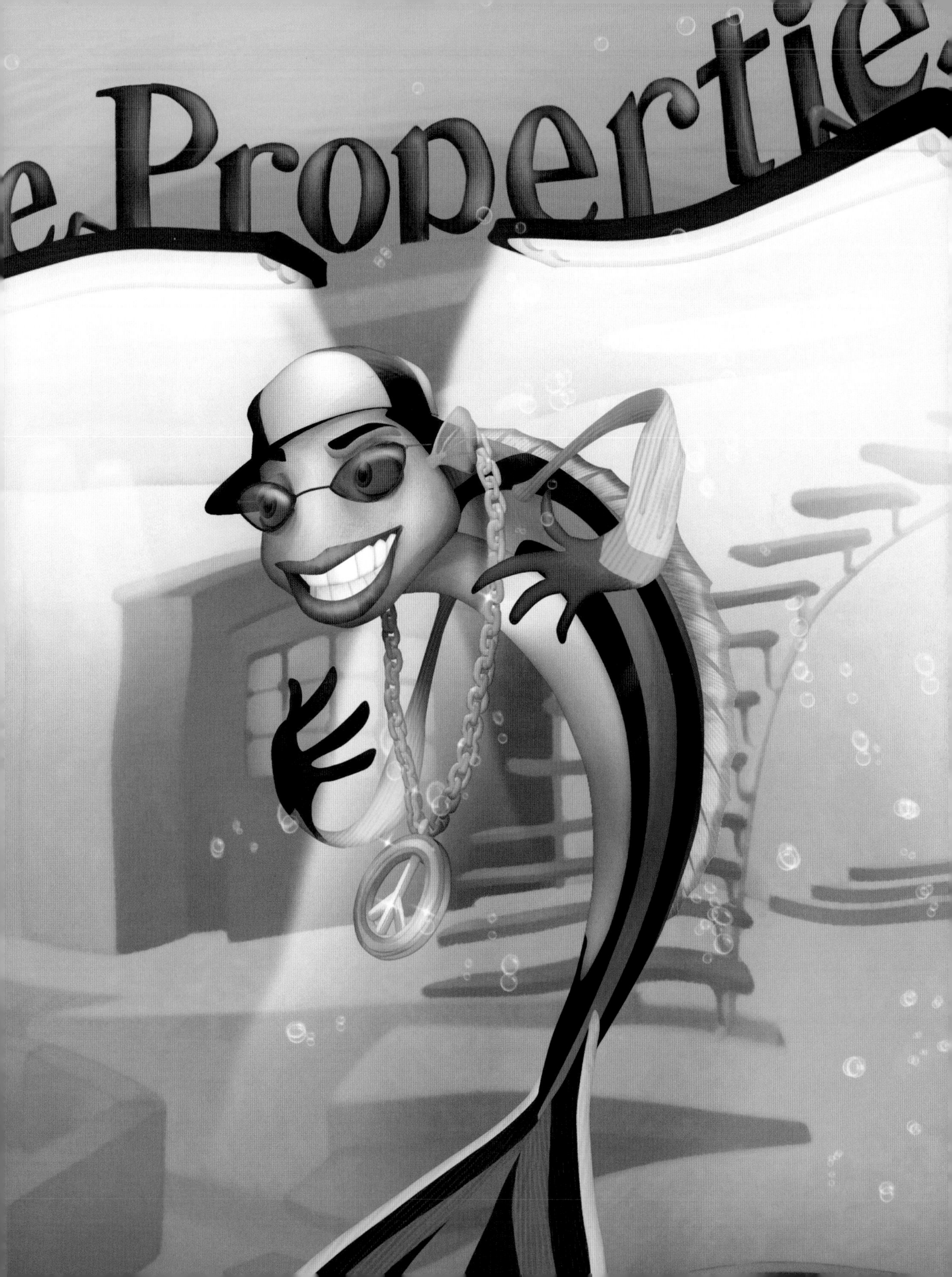
e Propertie

At the Whale Wash, Oscar went straight to Angie's booth.
He twirled her around and danced.

Angie laughed at his hip-hop moves. "You're late . . . again."

"C'mon, Ange." Oscar grinned, handing her a bag of doughnuts.
"I'm gonna be rich one day soon – I don't need this job!"

Angie clapped her fins over her ears. "I am not even going to
listen to you!"

Oscar swam out of the booth, laughing and dancing his way
through the wash.

At every station, he taught the workers a new move. By the time
he reached his boss's office, the Whale Wash was grooving to his
Oscarlicious rhythm.

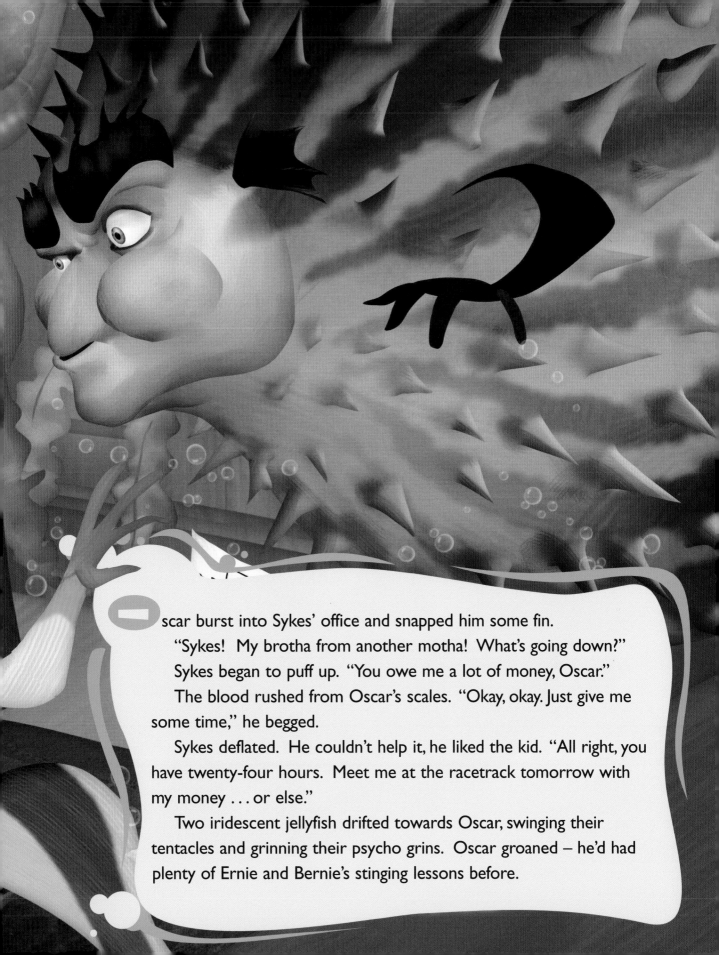

Oscar burst into Sykes' office and snapped him some fin.

"Sykes! My brotha from another motha! What's going down?"

Sykes began to puff up. "You owe me a lot of money, Oscar."

The blood rushed from Oscar's scales. "Okay, okay. Just give me some time," he begged.

Sykes deflated. He couldn't help it, he liked the kid. "All right, you have twenty-four hours. Meet me at the racetrack tomorrow with my money . . . or else."

Two iridescent jellyfish drifted towards Oscar, swinging their tentacles and grinning their psycho grins. Oscar groaned – he'd had plenty of Ernie and Bernie's stinging lessons before.

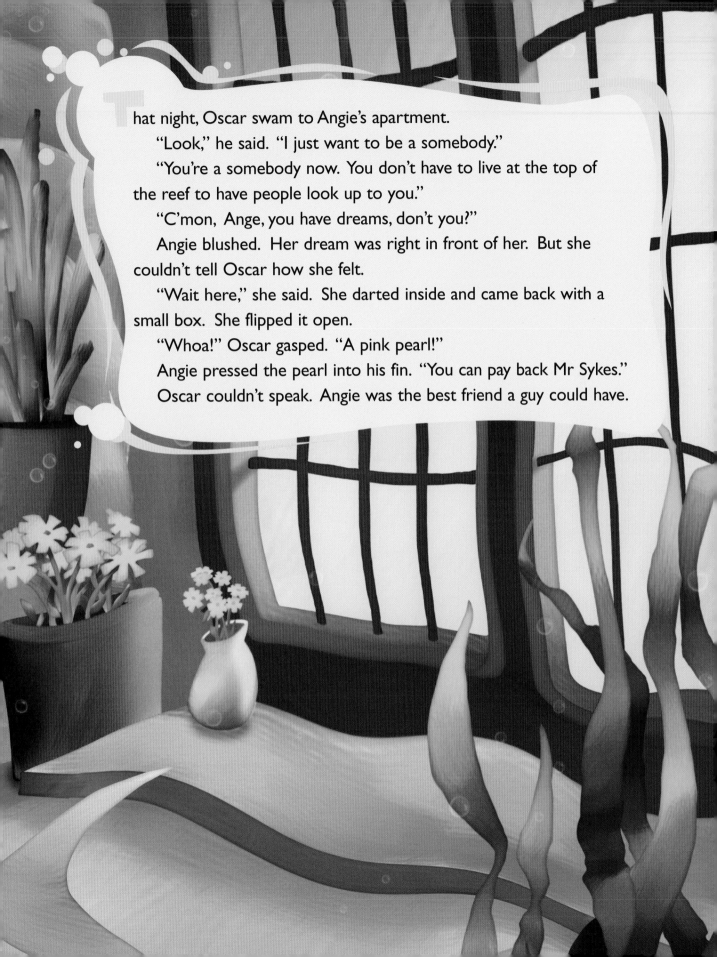

That night, Oscar swam to Angie's apartment.

"Look," he said. "I just want to be a somebody."

"You're a somebody now. You don't have to live at the top of the reef to have people look up to you."

"C'mon, Ange, you have dreams, don't you?"

Angie blushed. Her dream was right in front of her. But she couldn't tell Oscar how she felt.

"Wait here," she said. She darted inside and came back with a small box. She flipped it open.

"Whoa!" Oscar gasped. "A pink pearl!"

Angie pressed the pearl into his fin. "You can pay back Mr Sykes."

Oscar couldn't speak. Angie was the best friend a guy could have.

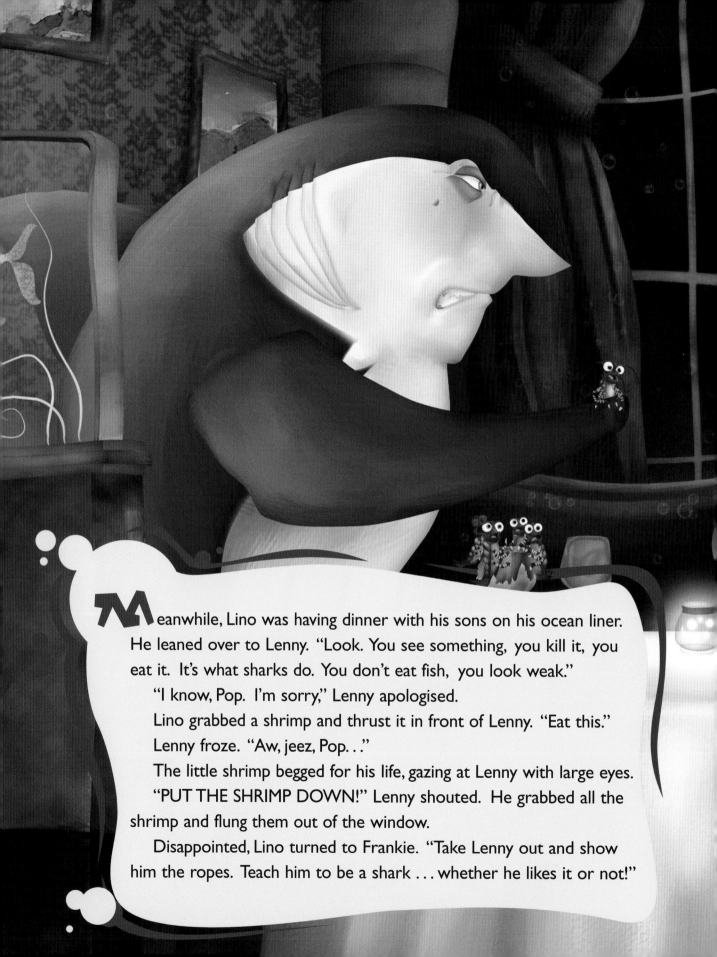

Meanwhile, Lino was having dinner with his sons on his ocean liner. He leaned over to Lenny. "Look. You see something, you kill it, you eat it. It's what sharks do. You don't eat fish, you look weak."

"I know, Pop. I'm sorry," Lenny apologised.

Lino grabbed a shrimp and thrust it in front of Lenny. "Eat this."

Lenny froze. "Aw, jeez, Pop. . ."

The little shrimp begged for his life, gazing at Lenny with large eyes.

"PUT THE SHRIMP DOWN!" Lenny shouted. He grabbed all the shrimp and flung them out of the window.

Disappointed, Lino turned to Frankie. "Take Lenny out and show him the ropes. Teach him to be a shark . . . whether he likes it or not!"

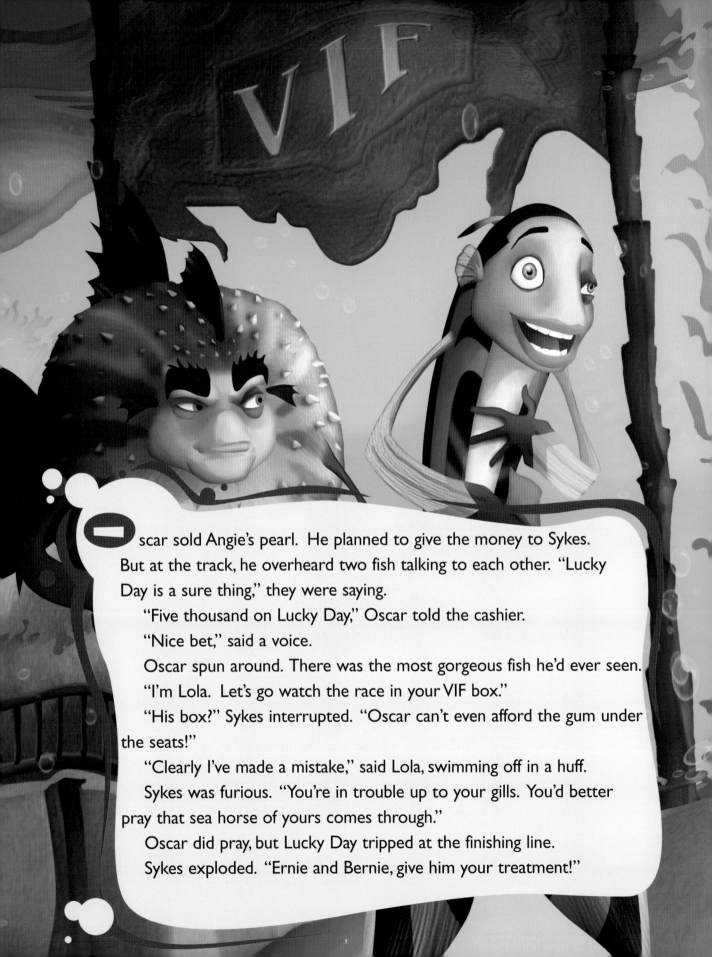

Oscar sold Angie's pearl. He planned to give the money to Sykes. But at the track, he overheard two fish talking to each other. "Lucky Day is a sure thing," they were saying.

"Five thousand on Lucky Day," Oscar told the cashier.

"Nice bet," said a voice.

Oscar spun around. There was the most gorgeous fish he'd ever seen.

"I'm Lola. Let's go watch the race in your VIF box."

"His box?" Sykes interrupted. "Oscar can't even afford the gum under the seats!"

"Clearly I've made a mistake," said Lola, swimming off in a huff.

Sykes was furious. "You're in trouble up to your gills. You'd better pray that sea horse of yours comes through."

Oscar did pray, but Lucky Day tripped at the finishing line.

Sykes exploded. "Ernie and Bernie, give him your treatment!"

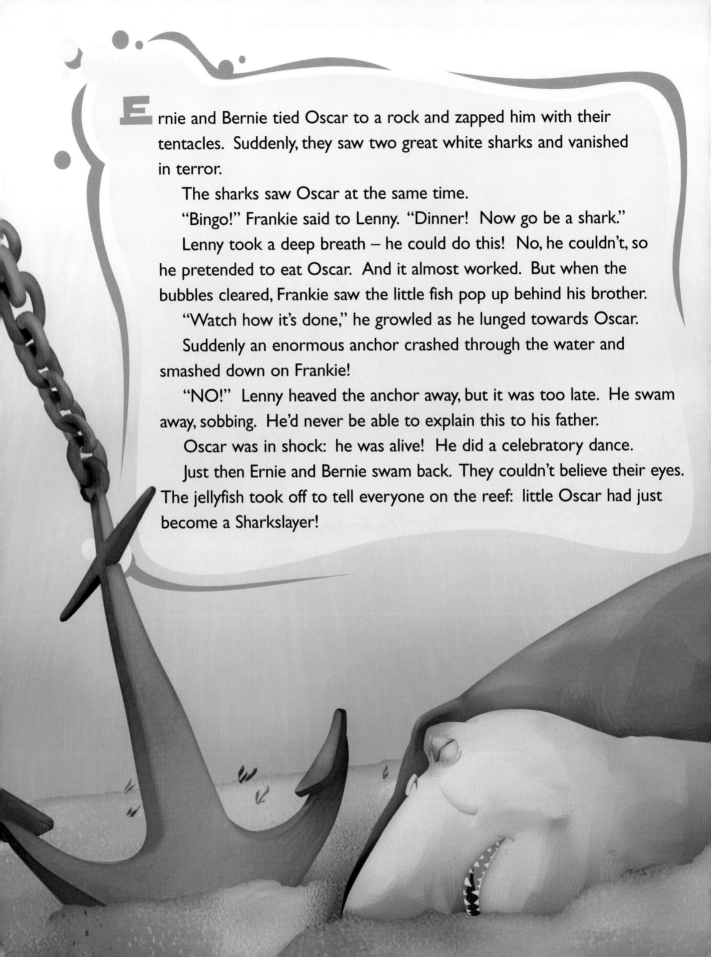

Ernie and Bernie tied Oscar to a rock and zapped him with their tentacles. Suddenly, they saw two great white sharks and vanished in terror.

The sharks saw Oscar at the same time.

"Bingo!" Frankie said to Lenny. "Dinner! Now go be a shark."

Lenny took a deep breath – he could do this! No, he couldn't, so he pretended to eat Oscar. And it almost worked. But when the bubbles cleared, Frankie saw the little fish pop up behind his brother.

"Watch how it's done," he growled as he lunged towards Oscar.

Suddenly an enormous anchor crashed through the water and smashed down on Frankie!

"NO!" Lenny heaved the anchor away, but it was too late. He swam away, sobbing. He'd never be able to explain this to his father.

Oscar was in shock: he was alive! He did a celebratory dance.

Just then Ernie and Bernie swam back. They couldn't believe their eyes. The jellyfish took off to tell everyone on the reef: little Oscar had just become a Sharkslayer!

ord spread like a tidal wave. Within hours, Oscar was the biggest
hero in the city . . . television interviews, magazine covers, parties all
over town. The Whale Wash went wild with excitement.

"I'll be your manager," announced Sykes. "We're gonna make a
fortune!"

Oscar was heading straight for the top of the reef, right where a
Sharkslayer belonged. Except, of course, he hadn't actually killed a shark.
But nobody knew that.

t Frankie's funeral, word rippled through the crowd.

    The tiger sharks whispered to the sawtooths, and the makos mumbled to the hammerheads: a Sharkslayer had killed Frankie.

    While his family wept, Don Lino vowed revenge.

    "I'm gonna find this Sharkslayer!" he swore to the mourners who came to pay their respects.

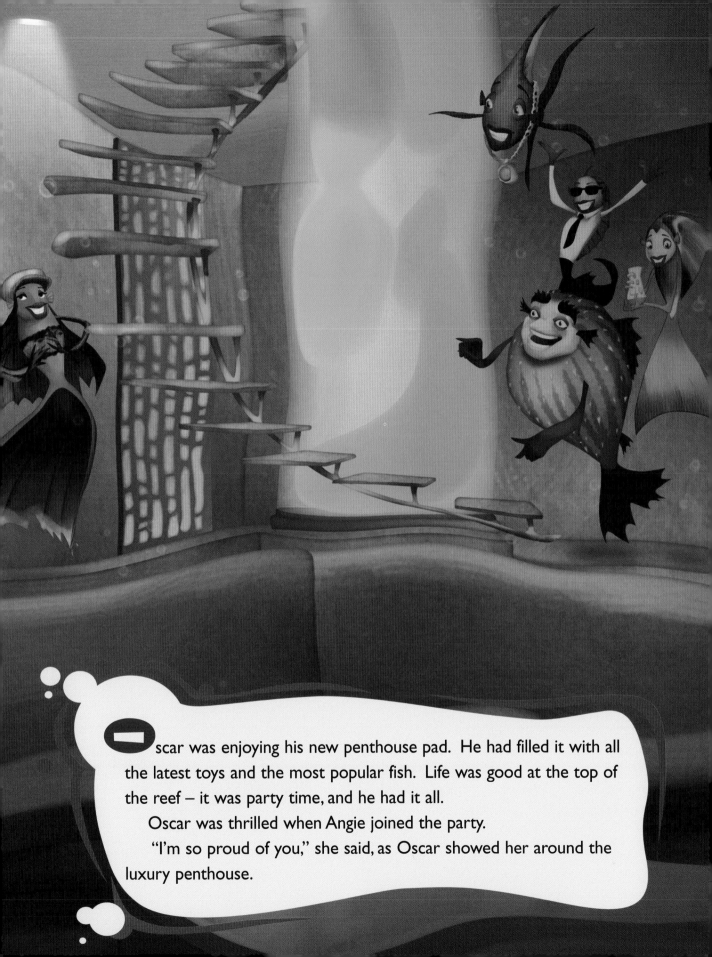

Oscar was enjoying his new penthouse pad. He had filled it with all the latest toys and the most popular fish. Life was good at the top of the reef – it was party time, and he had it all.

Oscar was thrilled when Angie joined the party.

"I'm so proud of you," she said, as Oscar showed her around the luxury penthouse.

"Angie, I couldn't have done it without you," Oscar told her. He held out a small box. Inside was Angie's pink pearl, strung into a necklace with dozens of others!

Before Angie could thank him, Lola shimmied over.

"Looks like you're a somebody now!" She linked her fin in Oscar's and swam him away from Angie.

Just then a frightened fish swam into the room. "Sharks! At the edge of the reef!" he cried.

Everyone turned to Oscar. He froze.

There was no choice . . . he'd have to act like a Sharkslayer.

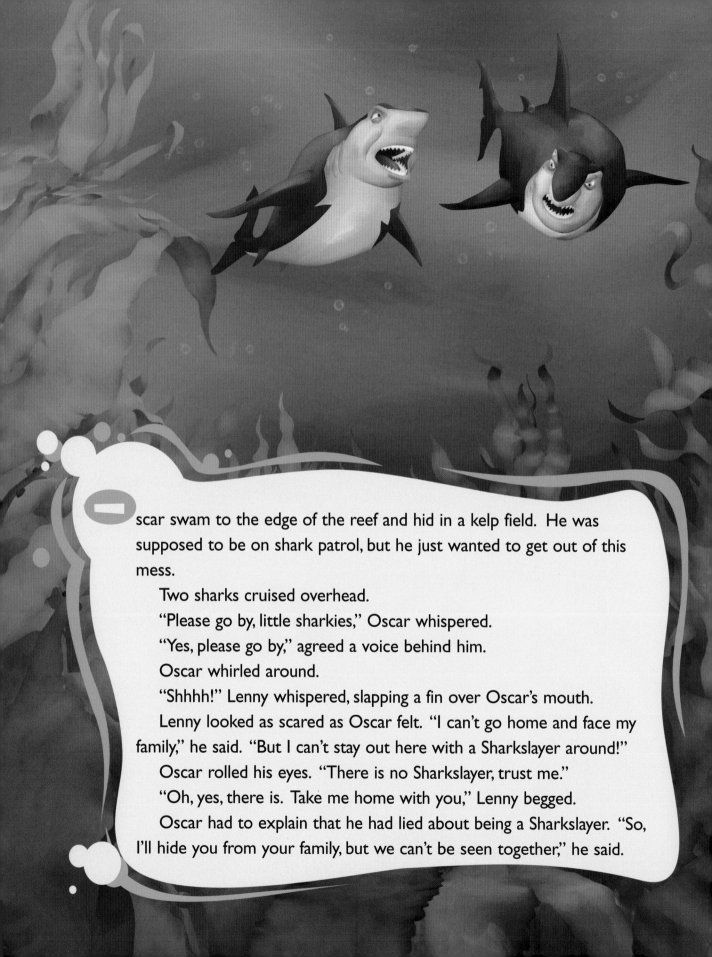

scar swam to the edge of the reef and hid in a kelp field. He was supposed to be on shark patrol, but he just wanted to get out of this mess.

Two sharks cruised overhead.

"Please go by, little sharkies," Oscar whispered.

"Yes, please go by," agreed a voice behind him.

Oscar whirled around.

"Shhhh!" Lenny whispered, slapping a fin over Oscar's mouth.

Lenny looked as scared as Oscar felt. "I can't go home and face my family," he said. "But I can't stay out here with a Sharkslayer around!"

Oscar rolled his eyes. "There is no Sharkslayer, trust me."

"Oh, yes, there is. Take me home with you," Lenny begged.

Oscar had to explain that he had lied about being a Sharkslayer. "So, I'll hide you from your family, but we can't be seen together," he said.

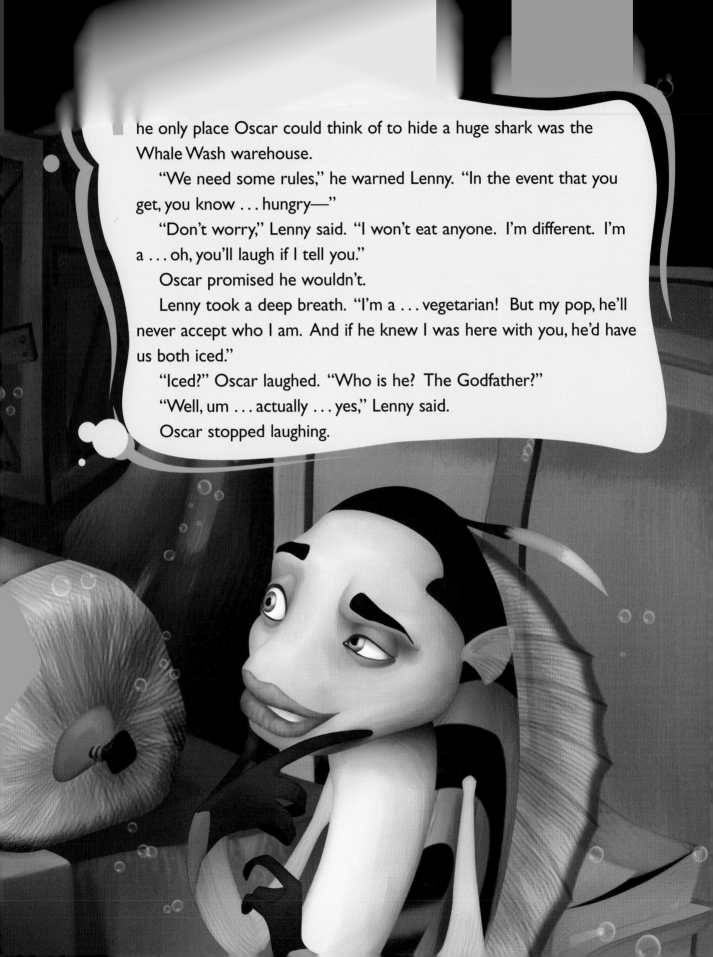

he only place Oscar could think of to hide a huge shark was the Whale Wash warehouse.

"We need some rules," he warned Lenny. "In the event that you get, you know . . . hungry—"

"Don't worry," Lenny said. "I won't eat anyone. I'm different. I'm a . . . oh, you'll laugh if I tell you."

Oscar promised he wouldn't.

Lenny took a deep breath. "I'm a . . . vegetarian! But my pop, he'll never accept who I am. And if he knew I was here with you, he'd have us both iced."

"Iced?" Oscar laughed. "Who is he? The Godfather?"

"Well, um . . . actually . . . yes," Lenny said.

Oscar stopped laughing.

Oscar raced back to his penthouse. "Sykes, we're in big trouble, man! That shark I killed was Don Lino's son! What if he finds out?"

"He already knows, and you should see how mad he is!" Sykes began to puff up in excitement. "He's sending a pack of his boys after you tomorrow morning. You can slay 'em all! You're gonna be even more famous, and we're gonna cash in big time!"

Oscar tried not to panic, but he needed a plan – fast.

Angie was at the warehouse when Oscar arrived. Lenny had told her everything.

"You lied to me, Oscar," she said. "How could you do that?"

"I lied to everyone, Angie. I'm really sorry. But now I've got this little problem ... SHARKS ARE COMING TO GET ME!" He turned to Lenny. "They're looking for you, too. We've gotta come up with a plan."

Angie tried to convince them both to just tell the truth, but Oscar and Lenny weren't interested.

"Okay. You need to slay a shark," Lenny said to Oscar. "And I need to disappear. What if we pretend ...?"

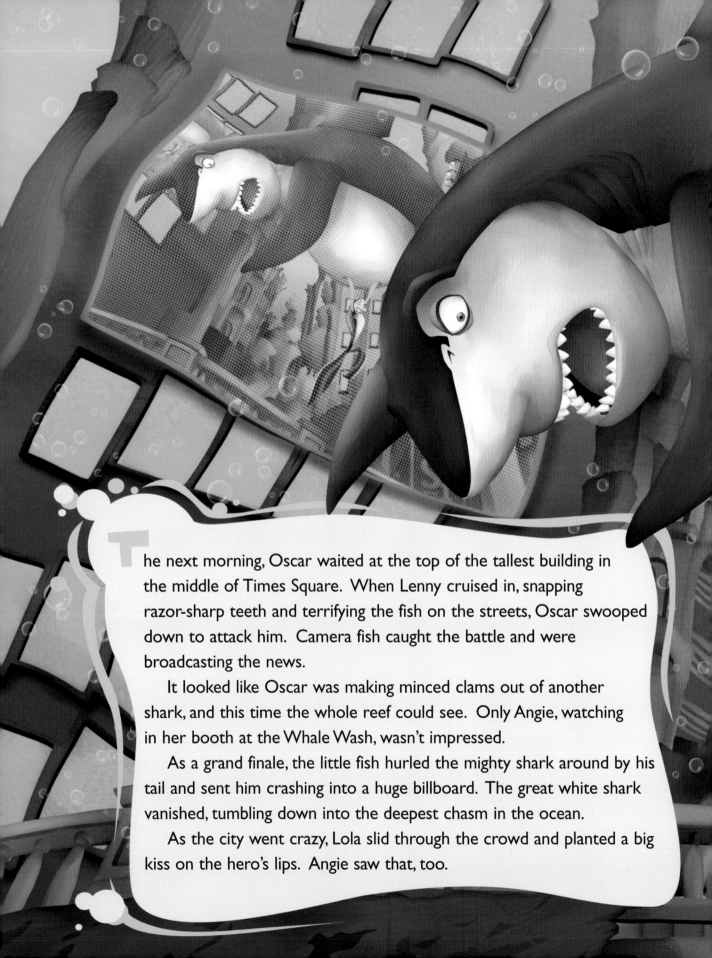

The next morning, Oscar waited at the top of the tallest building in the middle of Times Square. When Lenny cruised in, snapping razor-sharp teeth and terrifying the fish on the streets, Oscar swooped down to attack him. Camera fish caught the battle and were broadcasting the news.

It looked like Oscar was making minced clams out of another shark, and this time the whole reef could see. Only Angie, watching in her booth at the Whale Wash, wasn't impressed.

As a grand finale, the little fish hurled the mighty shark around by his tail and sent him crashing into a huge billboard. The great white shark vanished, tumbling down into the deepest chasm in the ocean.

As the city went crazy, Lola slid through the crowd and planted a big kiss on the hero's lips. Angie saw that, too.

When Oscar danced into the warehouse later,
Angie was fuming.

"Lola is only interested in you because you're rich
and famous!"

"She treats me like a somebody!" Oscar said. "Nobody loved
me when I was a nobody!"

"I did!" Angie blurted out.

Oscar and Angie stared at each other in surprise.

Just then Lenny appeared. He had spray-painted himself blue and
squeezed his snout tight with rubber bands. "Ta-da! Sebastian the
dolphin! How do you like my disguise?"

Oscar and Angie kept staring at each other. Finally Angie turned away.

"Oh, just go back to your great life, Oscar," she said. "So I can get on
with mine."

Oscar swam home. He didn't feel much like a hero any more.

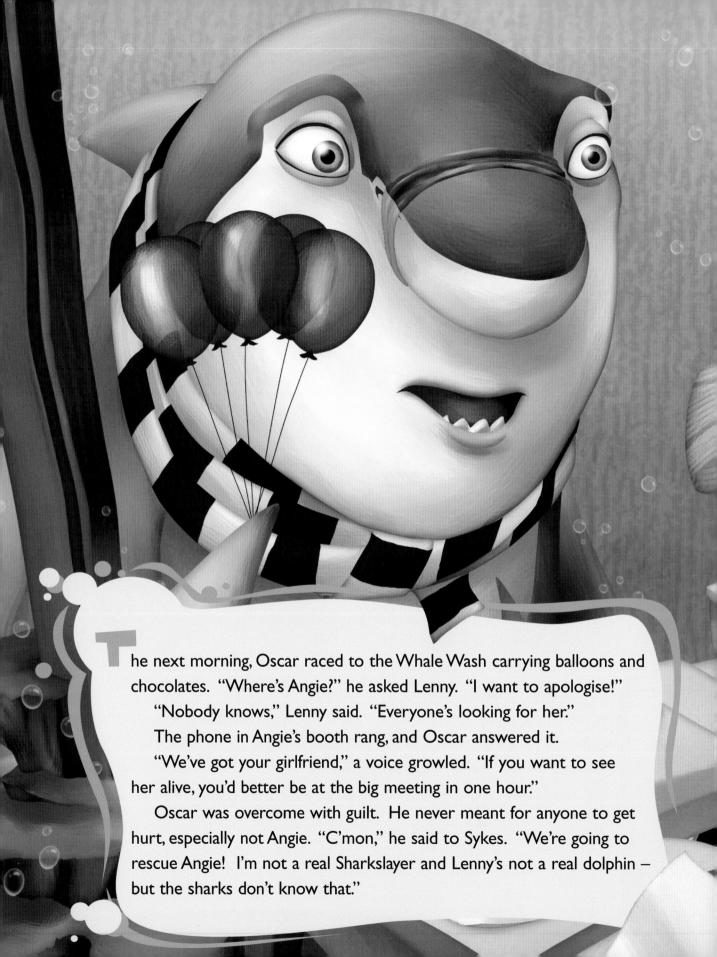

The next morning, Oscar raced to the Whale Wash carrying balloons and chocolates. "Where's Angie?" he asked Lenny. "I want to apologise!"

"Nobody knows," Lenny said. "Everyone's looking for her."

The phone in Angie's booth rang, and Oscar answered it.

"We've got your girlfriend," a voice growled. "If you want to see her alive, you'd better be at the big meeting in one hour."

Oscar was overcome with guilt. He never meant for anyone to get hurt, especially not Angie. "C'mon," he said to Sykes. "We're going to rescue Angie! I'm not a real Sharkslayer and Lenny's not a real dolphin – but the sharks don't know that."

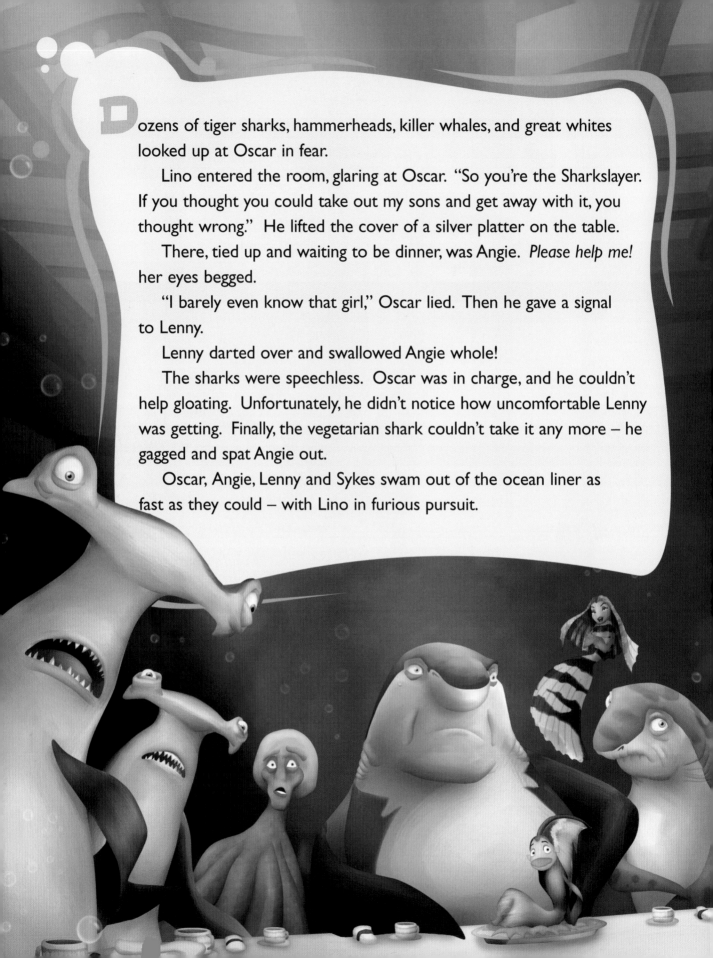

ozens of tiger sharks, hammerheads, killer whales, and great whites looked up at Oscar in fear.

Lino entered the room, glaring at Oscar. "So you're the Sharkslayer. If you thought you could take out my sons and get away with it, you thought wrong." He lifted the cover of a silver platter on the table.

There, tied up and waiting to be dinner, was Angie. *Please help me!* her eyes begged.

"I barely even know that girl," Oscar lied. Then he gave a signal to Lenny.

Lenny darted over and swallowed Angie whole!

The sharks were speechless. Oscar was in charge, and he couldn't help gloating. Unfortunately, he didn't notice how uncomfortable Lenny was getting. Finally, the vegetarian shark couldn't take it any more – he gagged and spat Angie out.

Oscar, Angie, Lenny and Sykes swam out of the ocean liner as fast as they could – with Lino in furious pursuit.

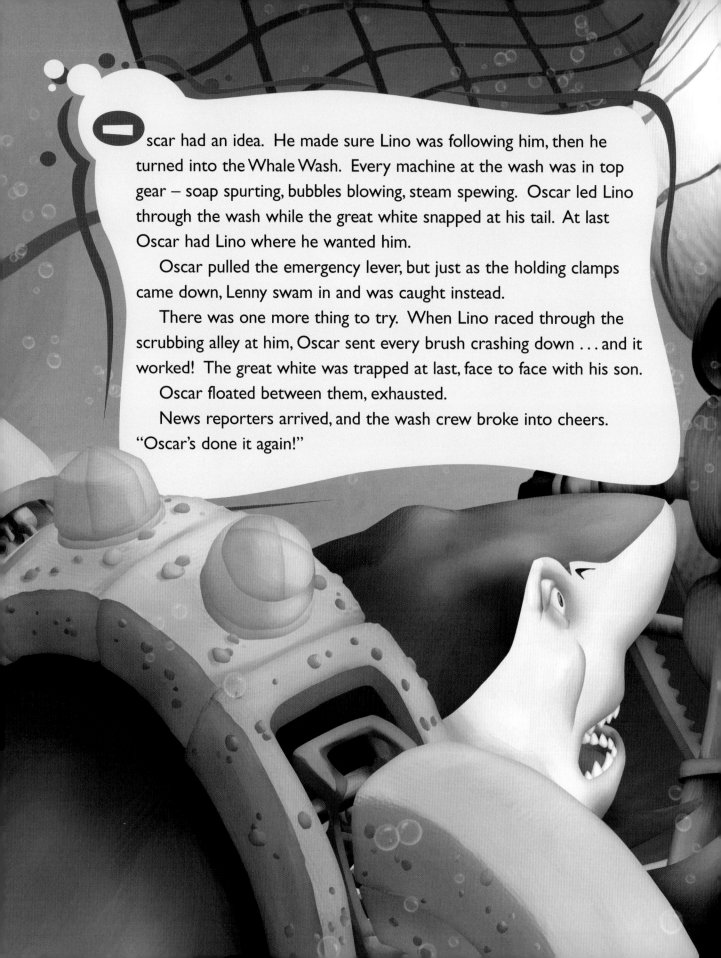

scar had an idea. He made sure Lino was following him, then he turned into the Whale Wash. Every machine at the wash was in top gear – soap spurting, bubbles blowing, steam spewing. Oscar led Lino through the wash while the great white snapped at his tail. At last Oscar had Lino where he wanted him.

Oscar pulled the emergency lever, but just as the holding clamps came down, Lenny swam in and was caught instead.

There was one more thing to try. When Lino raced through the scrubbing alley at him, Oscar sent every brush crashing down . . . and it worked! The great white was trapped at last, face to face with his son.

Oscar floated between them, exhausted.

News reporters arrived, and the wash crew broke into cheers. "Oscar's done it again!"

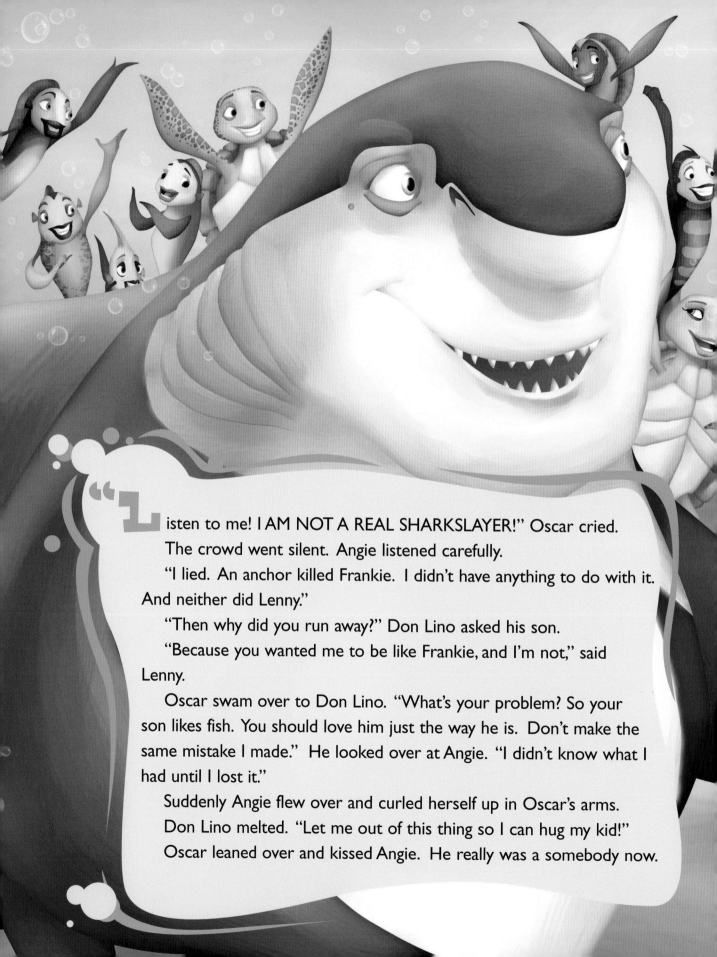

"Listen to me! I AM NOT A REAL SHARKSLAYER!" Oscar cried.

The crowd went silent. Angie listened carefully.

"I lied. An anchor killed Frankie. I didn't have anything to do with it. And neither did Lenny."

"Then why did you run away?" Don Lino asked his son.

"Because you wanted me to be like Frankie, and I'm not," said Lenny.

Oscar swam over to Don Lino. "What's your problem? So your son likes fish. You should love him just the way he is. Don't make the same mistake I made." He looked over at Angie. "I didn't know what I had until I lost it."

Suddenly Angie flew over and curled herself up in Oscar's arms.

Don Lino melted. "Let me out of this thing so I can hug my kid!"

Oscar leaned over and kissed Angie. He really was a somebody now.

A new day at the Whale Wash. Oscar was the manager and he had a plan – for a party! Sharks, fish, turtles . . . everyone wanted to be at the Whale Wash. They were all working, dancing and having a good time.

Get with it with these other *Shark Tale* titles:

Movie Novel

Hip Hop 'Til You Flop

Joke Book

Scholastic Children's Books
Commonwealth House, 1-19 New Oxford Street
London WC1A 1NU, UK
a division of Scholastic Ltd
London ~ New York ~ Toronto ~ Sydney ~ Auckland
Mexico City ~ New Delhi ~ Hong Kong

First published in the USA by Scholastic Inc., 2004
First published in the UK by Scholastic Ltd, 2004

DreamWorks' Shark Tale TM and © 2004 DreamWorks L.L.C.

ISBN 0 439 96353 2

Printed by Proost, Belgium

2 4 6 8 10 9 7 5 3 1